POPPY THE PEA

Oh, what a great way to be.

To Nicky + family

with my best wishes,

Dr. Fozz

30-11-23

Published lovingly by

Fuzz Books in London

POPPY THE PEA

Oh, what a great way to be.

Dr. Fuzz

The original and authorized first edition

ABOUT THE AUTHOR & ILLUSTRATOR

Farzad Sharifi-Yazdi grew up in Berkhamsted, England, where he picked up his enduring nickname, Fuzz, and his love of poetry. At fourteen, his national prize-winning poem, 'Brian's Head', was published in Britain's leading newspaper, *The Times*. Curiosity about a war that had distanced him from his birthplace, Iran, at the age of five, later inspired Farzad's doctorate in Geopolitics from King's College London. His first book, on Middle East rivalries and disputes, was published by Bloomsbury in 2015. Writing for children has been Farzad's long-held dream — what better way to promote mental health and international peace, subjects extremely dear to his heart. Farzad lives in London with his wife, Sarah, and cat, Maxi.

———◇———

Written & Illustrated by Farzad Sharifi-Yazdi

ISBN 978-1-7393909-0-7 (hardback)
ISBN 978-1-7393909-1-4 (ebook)
9 8 7 6 5 4 3 2 1

First edition July 2023
Book design — Clare Baggaley
Printed and bound by Oriental Press

For more information:
info@poppythepea.com
www.poppythepea.com

Dedicated to every sweet pea longing to be free.

زن، ذندگی، آزادی

Women. Life. Freedom

CHAPTER ONE

...in which we meet Poppy

———◇———

Poppy the Pea was a pea,

Sweet and green as could be.

Rather round like a ball,

Somewhat small, like a pea...

Oh, how lovely is she, I'm sure you'll agree!

Poppy was also a pea amongst peas,

Peas she called mates, many mates that were peas.

All somewhat small and in a tight squeeze,

Adrift in the dark and freezy degrees.

Oh, the life of sweet peas, in freezy degrees!

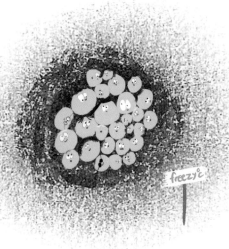

freezy'e

But Poppy the Pea was one of a kind,

The most unlikely pea you're likely to find.

With dreams in her heart and fears in her mind,

The fears always foremost, dreams trailing behind.

Oh, the dreams of your heart and fears of your mind!

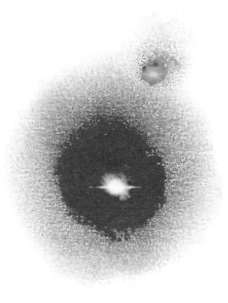

Now, the fear that Poppy feared quite the most

Was not that of a knife, nor a fork, nor a roast.

No, the thought of bright light scared Poppy utmost,

It frightened her more than monsters and ghosts!

Oh, it's your thoughts that can frighten the most!

But why, you may ask, did Poppy fear light?

Well, 'twas a mystery full of possible frights.

All she knew was the dark and the colours of night.

Dreaming in comfort, keeping well out of sight.

Oh, staying in comfort can keep fright alight!

And yet, at the same time, Poppy the Pea,

Was a pea who dreamed dreams enormously,

With a dream above all to be bold like a tree,

And forever roll onwards, free as a bee.

Oh, to be bold as a tree and free as a bee!

Now, it's worth noting before it's too late,

And in case you're curious and keen to relate,

That Poppy's dream was inspired by Percy the Great,

A pea so **bold** he had leapt from a plate!

*Oh, the remarkable legend of Percy the Great
(back in the year 1888)!*

Stories were told of this pioneer pea,

Of where he'd been, what he went on to see.

And these stories dazzled our Poppy the Pea,

Sparked her dream to be bold, her urge to roll free.

Oh, the stories that dazzle, inspire you to be!

'Dazzling'
THE NEW FEATURES.

'Inspiring'
THE DAILY PERSEUM.

THE ADVENTURES
OF
PERCY THE GREAT
MMX

Alas, Poppy's dream seemed somewhat impossible,

So far out of reach and highly improbable,

For her fear felt immense, truly immovable,

Thoughts of facing it all were simply intolerable.

Oh, how your dreams can be so very vulnerable!

Intolerable!
Immovable!
Improbable!
Impossible!

But all of this changed at a zippy-zap rate,

One certain lunchtime at 12:28,

When Poppy awoke to face a new fate:

From dark freezer to pan, from hot pan to bright plate!

Oh, how quickly things pass, how swiftly things change!

CHAPTER TWO
...in which Poppy peeps

———◇———

Poppy squeezed her eyes shut as she sat on the plate,

She was in quite a bother, she was in quite a state.

Her fear, out of five, was about fifty-eight!

The bright light was upon her, like a hunter in wait...

Oh, when your fear feels gigantic, simply too great!

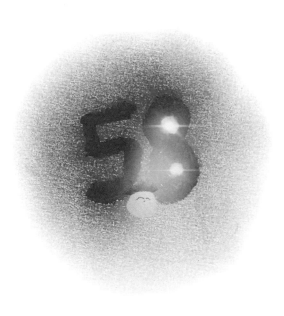

But then came the hum and hymn of her mates:

"Oh, the tummy-tum-tum, such a warm cosy space,

We're off to a tummy, tum-tummies are ace!"

"Poppy," one whispered, "sing along and embrace!"

Oh, the joys of hearing from jolly good mates!

"Embrace?" cried Poppy, confused and dismayed.

"Yes," replied Petey, Poppy's trusted best mate.

"It's about facing it all – even if you're afraid,

The bad, the sad, the things that you hate."

Oh, facing it all - that's how heroes are made!

it's about facing it all!

Petey's whisper was soft but landed with weight

And stirred up the voice of Percy the Great:

"Poppy, open your eyes, let your heart lead the way,

Take charge of this moment, take charge of your fate!"

Oh, to follow your dream, it's never too late!

As her heart heard her hero having his say,

Poppy peeped at the fear that stood in her way,

Catching sight of the light, the brightness of day,

And how, as she did, fear cut short its stay!

Oh, look fear in the face, feel it flutter away!

CHAPTER THREE

...in which Poppy leaps

———◇———

Though tempted to join the *hurrahs* and *hurrays*,

Poppy's dream, she believed, was now hers to chase.

Feeling feisty and brave she farewelled with great haste,

Then took a deep breath and … leapt from the plate!

Oh, sometimes it takes brave leaps of faith!

Hurrah Hooray!

But where was she going? What was the plan?

To leap for the stars or to roll to Japan?

No, Poppy was heading where adventures began:

The firmly fixed ground, every inch, its full span!

Oh, to have a firm plan and believe that you can!

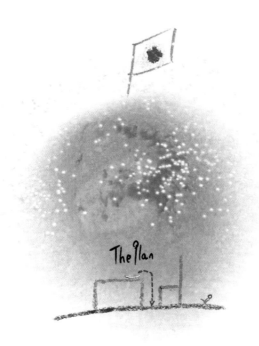

The Plan

But the ground is no place for a pea from a pan.

Poppy, you can't, the ground is for man!

"Oh, but I will, and oh, yes I can,

I'm a pea from a pan but a pea with a plan."

Oh, yes you can, sweet pea with a plan!

Yes

You

Can!

Poppy soared northwards and skimmed the cool air,

Then hurtled south-eastwards, towards an old chair

(A westerly wind was blowing her there)!

What a perilous journey, a scary affair!

But she smiled through it all, let go of her cares.

Oh, enjoy the big journey, let go of your cares!

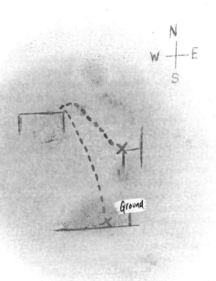

Ground

CHAPTER FOUR
...in which Poppy gets stuck

———◆———

Now, just as Poppy was getting the knack

Of falling with ease, of not looking back,

All things turned dimmer, then darker, then black

With a thumpity-bumpety, smackity-thwack!

Oh, there'll be knocks while you're getting the knack!

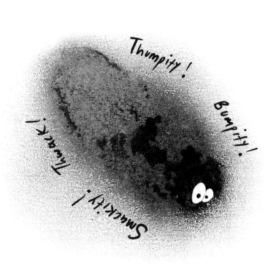

Thumpity!

Bumpity!

Thwack!

Smackity!

Poppy had wandered right off the sure track,

Bang onto a chair, into one little crack.

With no clear way out and no known way back,

This without doubt was a sticky setback!

Uh-oh, time to stage a stupendous comeback!

Safe Track

uh-oh!

This was not what she wanted, not Poppy's aim,

How could this happen and who was to blame?

"I shouldn't have jumped, I should have remained.

Now I'm stickity-stuck," she huffed and exclaimed.

Oh, your not-what-you-wants, your not-quite-your-aims!

And then: "Hello, sweet pea – my name is Jane,"

Said a small smiley spider sat on the chair frame.

"It's fine to feel anger, guilt and some shame,

These tricky feelings are just part of the game."

Oh, feeling your feelings is the name of the game!

"But I'm stickity-stuck," cried Poppy to Jane.

"What am I to do? It beats my pea brain."

"Chin up, sweet pea, and get pushing," said Jane.

"Just grab my web and let's go again."

Oh, we all need a Jane every now and again!

The web stuck to Poppy and she started to strain,

She wiggled and waggled, she felt through the pain.

And before she could say, "I thank you, sweet Jane!"

She swung into the light and was soaring again!

Oh, keep going, sweet pea, you're making good gain!

Keep going, Sweet Pea!

CHAPTER FIVE

...in which adventures begin

———◇———

What a sight to behold, as Poppy plunged down,

Tumbling aplenty, spinning around,

But not for one moment a fret or a frown,

As she finally landed on firm and fixed ground!

Oh, tumblings aplenty and landings abound!

Down on the floor and just a little bit sore,

Not long after lunchtime, at 1:44,

Poppy looked onto unbounded new shores.

Adventure was calling, 'twas time to explore!

Oh, exploring new shores is what you're built for!

And that my dear friends, I do hope you agree,

Is how we shall leave this unlikely pea:

Sweet and green as could be,

Rather round like a ball, somewhat small like a pea...

A pea with a dream dreamt enormously.

Who received words of wisdom heartfully.

Who faced fear and setback heroically.

And now rolling onwards, a pioneer pea...

Beautifully bold, finally free.

Oh, Poppy the Pea, what a great way to be!

The end
(for now...)